To Georgia
—B. M.

To Dad
—L. F.

Margaret K. McElderry Books
An imprint of Simon & Schuster Children's Publishing Division
1230 Avenue of the Americas
New York, NY 10020

Book design by Nina Barnett
The text of this book is set in Cheltenham Light.
The illustrations are rendered in pastel, colored pencils, and guoache paint.

Printed in Hong Kong

10 9 8 7 6 5 4 3 2 1

Library of Congress Catalog Card Number: 97-75775
ISBN 0-689-82085-2

FIRST
EDITION

My Bear and Me

by
BARBARA MAITLAND

pictures by
LISA FLATHER

Margaret K. McElderry Books

My Bear.
He's with me when I'm up,

and he's with me

when I'm down.

He's with me when it rains, and he's with me when the sun shines.

I'm never lonely when I'm with my Bear.

We sing together,

we swing together,

we walk together,

we talk together.

We ride together.

We even slide together!

When we're hungry, we eat,
and when we're thirsty, we drink.

When we're sleepy, we nap.

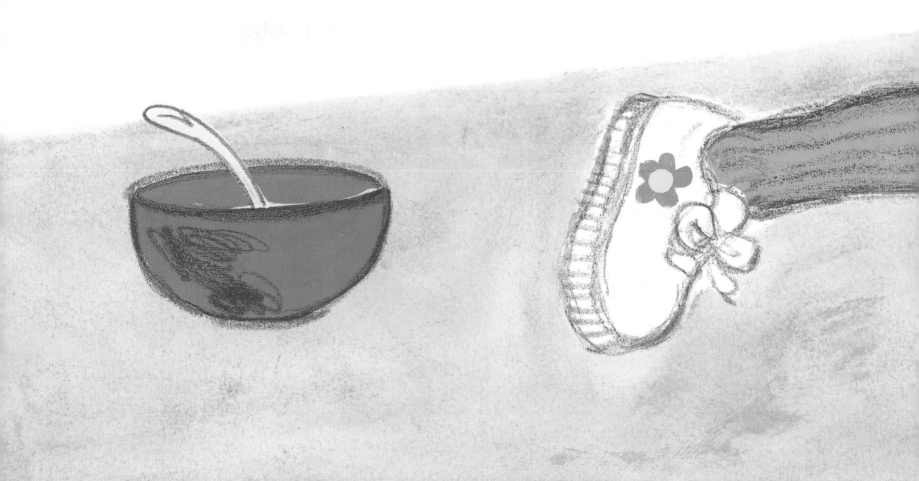

BUT . . .

you'd better watch out
when we're awake!

Ready or not,

here we come.

It's my Bear and me.

And at bedtime
when the lights go out,
and the door is
almost closed,
and I'm a little scared …

…my Bear is there,
safe and warm.

My Bear loves me

and I love my Bear.